I Want To Be Big

by Genie Iverson · pictures by David McPhail

A Unicorn Book

E. P. Dutton   New York

Library of Congress Cataloging in Publication Data

Iverson, Genie.   I want to be big.
(A Unicorn book)

SUMMARY: A little girl wishes she were big and able to
do all sorts of things but not big enough to have to
take care of herself all the time.
[1. Growth—Fiction]   I. McPhail, David M.   II. Title.
PZ7.I945Iae   1979   [E]   78-31101   ISBN: 0-525-32539-5

Published in the United States by E. P. Dutton, a Division
of Sequoia-Elsevier Publishing Company, Inc., New York

Published simultaneously in Canada by Clarke,
Irwin & Company Limited, Toronto and Vancouver

Editor: Emilie McLeod   Designer: Patricia Lowy
Printed in the U.S.A.   First Edition
10 9 8 7 6 5 4 3 2 1

For Pat and "Miska"

I want to be big.

I don't want to be big enough
to have to hang up my pajamas

but I do want to be big enough
to dress myself in the morning
as long as I get a little help
tying my shoes.

Not too big to hold my grandfather's hand
when we go for a walk

but big enough to cross the street by myself.

Big enough to take Caesar on a walk with my friends
instead of having Caesar take me for a walk with his.

Strong enough to make my swing go high
without anyone pushing me

but not so strong I go too high.

Big enough to know I have room
for another ice-cream cone

but not big enough to have room
for even one helping of peas.

Big enough to watch
a monster movie

but not too big
to have a night-light
and not too big
to scrunch under the covers.

Big enough so I can walk by myself
to the school bus in the morning
and be in the first grade

but not too big to visit
my kindergarten teacher.

I wish I were tall enough
to reach our fifth floor button in the elevator
so I wouldn't have to get out on four
and take the stairs.
And tall enough to spin my yo-yo
standing on the floor

but not too long to swim in the bathtub
or too tall to wear my old fuzzy bathrobe.

Big enough to eat dinner without
sitting on the telephone book

but not too big to sit
on my mother's lap for a story.

Too big to be spanked

but not big enough to give up my blanket.

Big enough to read my brother's
Spiderman comic books

but not too big to go
to story-hour at the library.

Big enough to eat dinner
at Mort's house

but not big enough
to spend the night.

Tall enough to reach my own cereal
when we go to the supermarket

but not too big
to fit on the bottom
of the shopping cart.

I'd like to be big enough
to help Mr. De Angelo weed and water
his vegetable garden on the roof

but not so grown-up
I have to drink
the cabbage juice he makes.

Big enough so my mother won't scold
when she sees me coming down the hall
with my giant see-through glass ant farm
with 500 worker ants

but not so big that she can say,
"You made that mess.
You clean it up." (Nobody's
big enough to catch 500 ants by herself.)

Not too big to help Ed
with the mail

but big enough to have
someone send me a letter.

 Not too big for my swimming pool

but big enough
to help get Cassius
down from the tree.

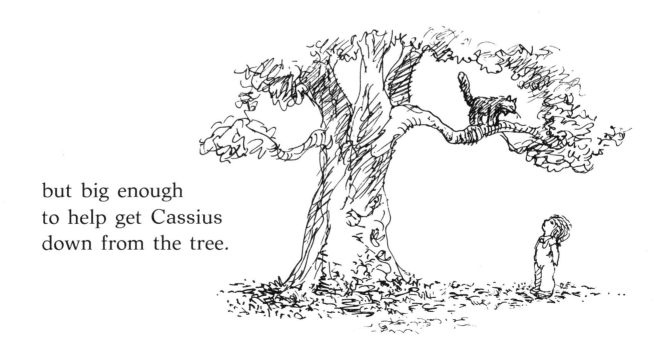

Big enough to make peanut butter
and jelly sandwiches for a picnic
but not so big I have to make
my own lunch for school.

Careful enough
to squirt whipped-cream roses
on my father's birthday cake
but not too big
to squirt a rose on Caesar.

Much too big for my party dress
with the itchy slip

but not too big for my vampire costume
with fangs and a black cape
and red spots like blood on the shirt.

Big enough to race my father
home from the corner

but not too big for a head start.

Tall enough to see the screen
instead of people's heads
when we go to the movies

but not too big
for a piggyback ride
on the way home.

Big enough to fix my own breakfast
when it's very early Sunday morning
and I'm hungry
and everybody is still asleep

and big enough to surprise
my mother and father
with cereal and juice
and the newspaper on a tray.

But not too big to crawl
under the covers with them
to read the funnies

or to start
a pillow fight.

I want to be big enough for a two-wheeler

with training wheels.

Big enough to take care of someone else
like Annabelle when she falls off her skateboard.
I'd put my arm around her and give her
my handkerchief and say, "Here. Blow."

Or my sister when she
sticks her arm out the hole
where her head is supposed to go.

But not quite big enough
to take care of myself all the time.

DATE DUE					
AUG 8 '92					
MAR 10 '93					
MAY 28					
AUG 10 1993					
FEB DEC					
SEP 25 1995					
DEC 02 1995					
FEB 08 1997					

HIGHSMITH 45-228